The Salmon Princess

An Alaska Cinderella Story   by Mindy Dwyer

PAWS IV
published by
Sasquatch Books

For Katey,
who never liked
salmon guts.

Manufactured in China in August 2013
by C&C Offset Printing Co. Ltd. Shenzhen,
Guangdong Province
Published by Sasquatch Books
17 16 15 14 13   15 14 13 12 11

Illustrations: Mindy Dwyer
Book Design: Stewart A. Williams

Library of Congress Cataloging-in-Publication
Data is available.

Sasquatch Books
1904 Third Avenue, Suite 710
Seattle, WA 98101
(206) 467-4300
www.sasquatchbooks.com
custserv@sasquatchbooks.com

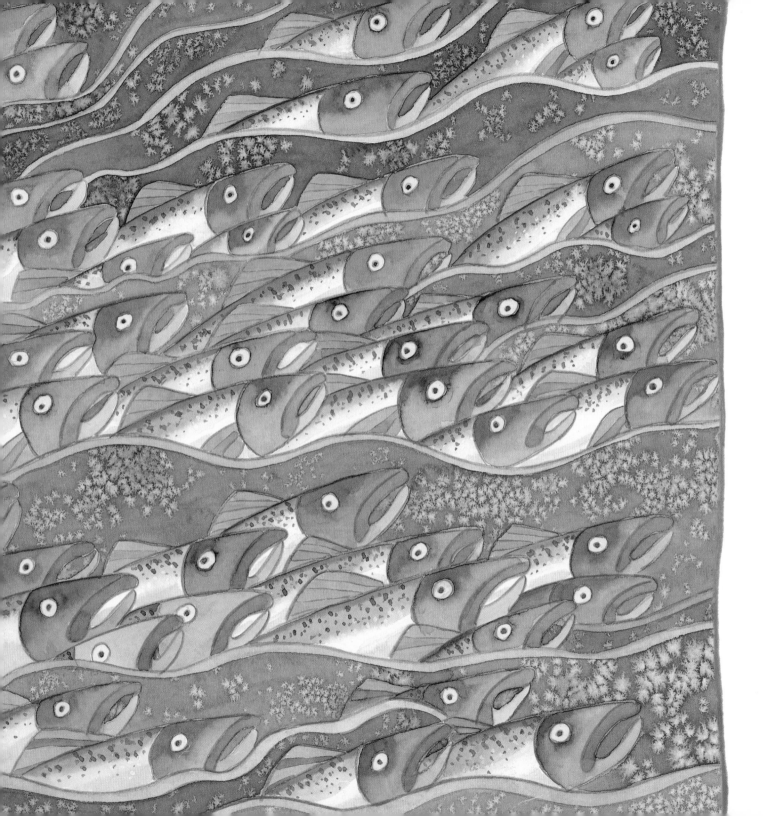

There once was
a place where a girl
could walk across the
sea on the backs of so
many wild salmon.

It was here in southeast Alaska, a fisherman, his wife, and their daughter called home. They lived at the edge of a shadowy rainforest where waterfalls made music with the drip-drip of the rain. It was a happy life, though it was full of hard work.

While the fisherman plucked fish from his nets, mother and daughter smoked salmon on the beach. Sweet smoke spiraled into the sky as they sang songs from long ago, a time when anything was possible.

One winter, the mother died suddenly. Cold rain poured from the sky. The daughter's tears ran rivers of sadness into the salty sea.

The fisherman held sadness in his heart like a great net bursting with fish.

Years passed and eventually the fisherman remarried. His new wife had two strong sons who quickly learned to catch fish. With three fishermen, the nets swelled with salmon. The stepmother refused to clean fish and gave that stinky, slimy job to the girl.

The girl's name was Cinder because of her smoky gray eyes that sparked like fire. Cinder had a favorite place in the forest at the base of an ancient cedar tree. She went there to smoke salmon the way her mother had taught her.

When the fisherman looked into his daughter's eyes, it wasn't the spark he saw, but the memory of the girl's mother looking at him. He buried his grief with more and more fish as the years drifted by.

One summer, the fisherman returned home with news of a Silver Salmon Festival on the mainland with a carousel, contests, and a dance followed by a raffle for a grand prize of real silver bars!

In all of the excitement, Cinder overheard her brothers talking about raffle tickets. They hoped to win the silver and buy a faster boat to catch more and more fish. If Cinder won the silver, *she* would not buy a salmon boat; she was already drowning in salmon! When Cinder asked to go to the festival, her stepmother said, "No! There are too many fish to clean!" Her father sadly said, "There are indeed all those fish."

She wanted to go to the dance more than anything she had ever wanted before. With the ease of a grizzly bear, she sliced all of the slippery salmon clean.

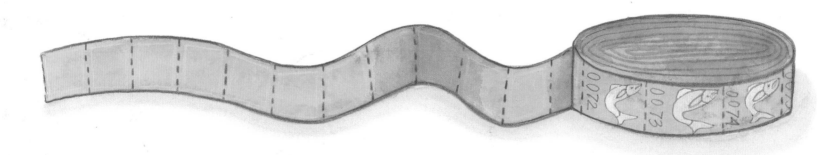

Cinder ran into the forest. "Even if I could go, I have nothing to wear to a dance, all of my clothes stink of fish guts," she thought.

Sitting under the cedar tree, she remembered her mother's sweet voice and began to sing softly. In the twilight she saw little silver stars peeking through the branches. She couldn't believe what she saw next!

An eagle dropped some-thing from the sky. A shim-mering salmon flopped on the ground at Cinder's feet.

As soon as she picked it up, she realized it was a shiny dress sewn with soft silver threads fit for a princess.

"Cinder," the eagle said, "Anything is possible. Go to the dance. But remember, you must return the dress before dawn. The silver will disappear in the light of day."

Cinder slipped into the silver dress and looked up to thank the eagle, but it was gone. Then she looked down at her Sitka Slippers, the heavy rubber boots that southeast Alaskans wore. Luckily, the dress covered her boots.

Wearing her new gown, Cinder headed to the festival. She remembered to bring some of her smoked salmon to sell so she could buy raffle tickets. Running toward the dock Cinder saw the brothers' fishing boat pull out into the bay. "I'll hop across on the swimming salmon if I have to," she vowed. Then, seeing the skiff, Cinder jumped in and started it up just as she had seen her father do a million times. The skiff pushed through the waves, its phosphorescent wake glowing like the train of a great wedding gown.

Oh, the Silver Salmon Festival was a sight more wonderful than a dream! Cinder had never seen such colorful lights. She saw a boy looking at her and her stomach flip-flopped just like a fish out of water. Their eyes met briefly but before the boy could ask for her name, she ran off to sell her salmon and then bought as many raffle tickets as she could.

Cinder found a long line of dancers and jumped in. When the boy saw the girl's wild red hair and smoky gray eyes that sparked he was hooked. Circling left, circling right, Cinder and her dance partner spun like the hands of the clock. In her long hair he smelled smoke as they twirled into the night.

At the glimmer of first light, Cinder suddenly remembered the eagle! She sprinted off the dance floor and down to the dock toward her skiff.

Her boot caught in a net and as she wrestled with it she dropped the raffle tickets. Cinder hopped into the skiff and hurried across the bay to return the dress, leaving her boot behind.

The boy followed her to the dock. First he found the lone boot and then the raffle tickets. But the girl was gone.

Back at the festival one of the girl's tickets held the winning number and there were only twenty-four hours to collect the prize! He had to find her. But, everyone wore those big rubber boots. It would be nearly impossible to find the match. The girl could be on any one of a hundred islands!

The boy searched every island and every bay and was about to give up when an eagle circling overhead led him to a dock.

On shore, he announced that he was looking for a girl with sparkling eyes who had won a prize. Cinder's father was confused and her stepmother laughed, "The only girl who lives here is covered in fish slime!"

Seeing a sparkle in their sister's eyes they'd never noticed before, Cinder's brothers locked her in the smokehouse and tried to think of a way to claim the prize.

Cinder fired up the old smoker and began to sing as smoke soared into the air. The boy followed the delightful song and sweet scent.

Unlocking the smokehouse door, he saw the girl he had been searching for. The boy smiled and Cinder's heart skipped like a smooth rock across water.

"Cinder?" her father called out, looking for her.

"Cinder? She's my Cinderella!" the boy cheered and offered her the boot.

It fit and Cinderella collected her prize of silver bars. She learned that the boy's father owned King Salmon Cannery. "So, that makes you a Salmon Prince!" she giggled.

When they married, Cinderella became the Salmon Princess and they lived happily ever after. Cinderella's stepmother was stuck cleaning salmon, so she went back to the Lower 48. The brothers ended up at the salmon cannery working long hard hours cleaning salmon. Cinderella forgave her father and he lived a long and happy fisherman's life on a healthy diet of salmon.

With the silver she'd won, Cinderella bought a homestead up north in the interior. She and the prince farmed prizewinning cabbages bigger than any salmon and had three daughters. Cinderella taught them to sing her mother's songs and to believe that anything is possible.

The Wedding

Uncles

Grandpa

The Homestead

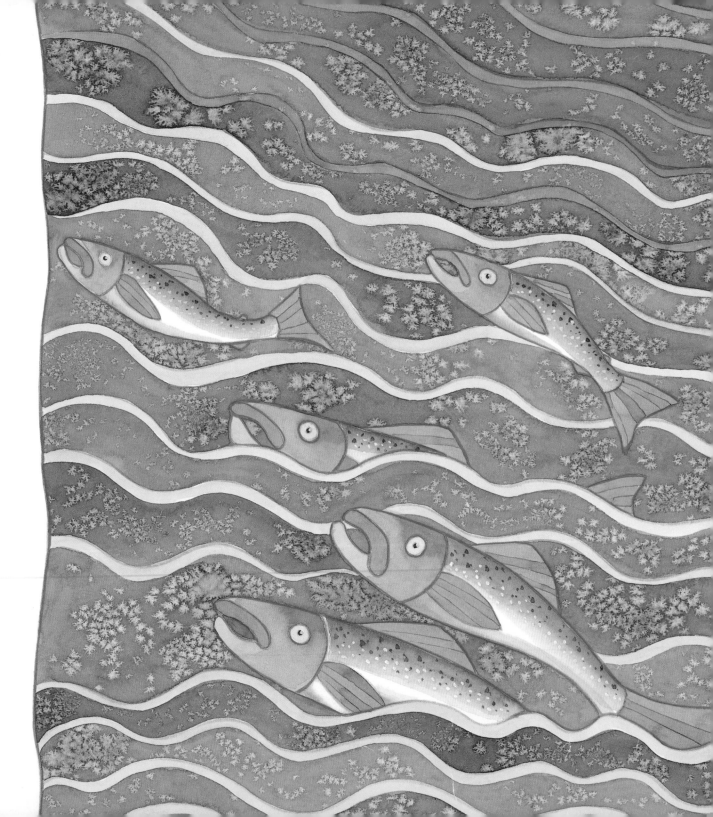

In time, the prince would take over his father's business at King Salmon and Cinderella believed that one day, they would all return home, just like the salmon.